Homemade Weather

An anthology of novelettes-in-flash

Edited by
Gaynor Jones

ISBN eBook: 978-1-9196087-0-9
ISBN print: 978-1-9196087-1-6

Retreat West Books
retreatwest.co.uk/books

Contents

What The Fox Brings In Its Jaw by Ian O'Brien

Foreword

ALL OF US at Retreat West are so excited to bring you this
first anthology of winning stories in the new annual
Novelette-in-Flash prize. These three winning novelettes
are simply stunning and achieve so much in so few words.
Each novelette is less than 8,000 words but contains the
breadth of human experience. The joy, pain, love and loss
experienced by these characters is brought to life in
stunning prose that demonstrates the sheer power of what
can be achieved with flash fiction.

Our thanks go to the judge of the 2020 contest,
Damhnait Monaghan, who had the toughest decision of
all to make. She said: 'These stories demonstrate the thin
line we tread in life: between love and hate, friendship and
enmity, escape and return, illness and recovery, life and
death. I was genuinely moved by each story.'

The winner of the first prize was Tom O'Brien for
Homemade Weather. Damhnait said: 'A beautifully
written, deeply satisfying novelette-in-flash that revealed
more depth with each read. A master class in both
resonance and the use of white space, with some of the
individual flash comprising a few sentences and one

having only a title and white space, to brilliant effect. Gorgeous lasting imagery and the promise of hope in the ambiguous ending. I could not get this story out of my head. A deserved winner.'

Second prize went to Ian O'Brien for *What The Fox Brings In Its Jaw*. Damhnait said: 'A constantly shifting narrative told from multiple perspectives, paired with the effective use of flashback helped elevate this excellent novelette-in-flash. An unnamed protagonist is caught up in a robbery that goes wrong, with tragic consequences. We see the impact of his poor choices on strangers, his own family and himself. It's a credit to the writer that the reader feels nothing but sympathy towards the man.'

Donna L Greenwood won third prize for *The Impossibility of Wings*. Damhnait said: In this fine novelette-in-flash, we witness a family in crisis, through the eldest daughter's eyes. Violent and erratic parental behaviour is leavened with humour and love – that fine line I referenced earlier. One of my favourite individual pieces in the competition is contained in this novelette. Bravo.'

We hope you enjoy these novelettes as much as we do.

Amanda Saint

Homemade Weather

Tom O'Brien

Book 1

First Sign

CELIA FINN. CELIA Finn. Celia Finn. I practice my signature, sitting on the chair outside the warped kitchen window. Scooping the e into the C, adding a tail to the F. Anything to not look at Ollie with his chin on his paws, too weak to lift his head while I explain that I don't want him to go. The lines in my copybook blur while Mam works on dinner inside. Condensation makes the glass weep.

Every one of Ollie's thin breaths whistles to the mountain across the valley, with its band of shadowed woods. When Dad told me the Jack Russell, nearly the same age as me, hadn't much time left, his hands moved like an axe cutting lines through the air. Some things on one side, some on the other.

I didn't want to hear what he said. No more than I want to hear the whispers at school, about him being mad for a game of pool on a weekend, how he loved to pot the red. The fake scandalised laughs, so I know they mean Casey's Bar and red headed Enda with the big hair who stands outside smoking by the yellow gas barrels even though that's so stupid. Fuck. When I swore out loud, the axe curled into a fist, but he didn't say a word. He's already said more than he would in a month. He thought it was only about the dog.

My throat hurts when Ollie closes his eyes.

He doesn't open them.

I concentrate on signing my name just right. When the tip leaves the paper, frozen pain screams up my arm and crushes my chest. The pen escapes from my hand. I twist from the chair after it until I'm on my back on the jabbing stones. My breath rises like snow clouds between me and the mountain while I flail from the perishing cold inside.

The clouds tinge red then black until Mam's baggy green socks are beside my face. She never wears shoes in the kitchen. Enda Casey would never wear socks like that with her heels and her hips and I can't breathe—

Mam holds my head, one hand chilled from running water over the potatoes. She slides me on to her kneeling lap and rocks me so I breathe in time with silent music.

I reach up but when my fingers touch her face she gasps and grabs the hand, then slips it inside her dress to give me her heat. The skin of her chest stiffens against my chilling touch.

'You're all right, loveen. You're all right,' she says, but as her warmth spreads to me I feel her clattering heart.

Behind her, Ollie yap, yap, yaps. Full of life.

The Father Daughter Talk

WHEN WE COME home from the doctor, Mam sends me to bed while she makes soup. It's only afternoon and the cover scratches my arm in disapproval.

Doctor O'Callaghan said there was nothing wrong with me, that I'd be right as ninepence, but I felt his peppermint breath turn from me when he sent a look to my mother. I caught the look above my distorted reflection on the stainless steel jug where he sterilises scissors and blades and things that press and pinch.

In my room my father is standing by the window. I didn't hear him come in or see him walk past me; only felt the air cool in his shadow.

'Do you see that mountain, Celia?'

I look where he's looking.

'It'll be there long after us, like it was before. No judgement.'

It seems like I should know what he means, but I don't, I never do.

However hard I look, I only see the mountain, and his shape in front of it.

The Squeaky Step

I SIT THREE steps from the top of the stairs so I can hear my parents in the kitchen without them knowing. When people do this on TV, they hear secrets, declarations of love, life-changing truths. I hear the silence behind my mother's humming.

When I search the air for her unasked questions, all I find is the kettle building from a hush to a scream.

'Why don't you talk to me?' she doesn't say.

As if in answer, my father turns a page of the Examiner, the rattle of it cracking like a lost opportunity.

The pour of the water from the kettle to the teapot, the wait for the dark tea to draw, is a ritual stripped of meaning.

'How do you think it's all right to go away on a Friday night and only come back when you feel like it?' goes without saying.

He stirs two spoons of sugar into his tea. Stainless steel on ceramic tinkles in an unbroken code.

'What kind of life is this?' she doesn't scream, 'For me, for Celia?' but he's had enough of this interrogation.

Taps a finger hard as a nail on the stained wood of the table.

I've heard all I'm going to hear and want to go back to my room, to close the door and hear only clean quiet, but I can't move without making a sound, so I sit on the step while my legs burn and the tea grows cold in the pot, trapped by the silence.

The Icing

BACK WHEN MAM would leave the house, we'd go to the Co-Op bakery behind the main store, to order my birthday cake. The round woman in the white coat and blue hairnet might be from a brochure or my memory, but the smell is the same sick sweet one rising from the bowl. Mam preheats the oven, lost in her kind-of-singing, her sort-of-music.

Cloud oozes over the mountain and across the valley. This autumn doesn't rain, but it's always wet.

'Icing,' I say, answering a question from years ago. 'And Smarties.'

Mam keeps humming, so I say it again.

'White icing for my birthday cake, and Smarties on top.'

The ghost of a tune surfaces and for a moment the sun breaks through and I'm in the car with her. The cake we'd ordered a week ago is on the back seat; I can taste the smell. The radio is on and the piped vinyl lines of the seat are sticky against the back of my legs. There's a green plastic strip across the top of the windscreen and I twist my hand in its light, watching how it changes my skin.

A horn beeps behind us, but we don't move. When I look, Mam is staring at someone on the street, someone I can't see. I have to tell her the lights have changed, that we have to go.

The next year she baked my cake at home and has done since.

My mother's private music blocks the silence, keeps a soft barrier between her and the things she might see or hear, inside or outside her head.

I can't see the mountain, lost in the low cloud, but I have to believe it's there.

Alarm

THE STUTTERING COUGH of the chainsaw rattles my bedroom window, shakes me awake. I have to remind my racing heart that the rising falling angry whine is just my father, back from town, starting work.

Predawn outlines the mountain, like he's cutting it from the sky.

I close my eyes until the roar of the blades fade down the valley, smothered by its gentle hush. But before I leave my bed, I wait for the bite of his axe to split the stillness.

This is how Dad comes home on a Monday. In the morning darkness, he attacks each trunk like it's the truth, breaking it into foot-long segments, chopping it apart to divide and conquer.

He won't come in for breakfast but raises an acknowledging arm that hides his face when I cycle from the yard. My tyres pick up sawdust and splinters that follow me to school, drawing a line on my back.

When I come back, he'll get me to help. Bagging logs, sealing them off. Splitting the small ones to kindling with my handaxe. If we talk, it won't break the silence.

Deals he made over the weekend turn up in late afternoon. Men with wind burned cheeks, fingers like split branches and work clothes that were once Sunday mass best shake his hand. They nod at me and at my mother through the kitchen window, not sure if it's her there or a reflection.

Before Dad comes into the house, he'll mix petrol and two-stroke for the chainsaw, measuring and pouring with a bartender's precision. He'll put the saw in the back of the van, along with the crosscut, the short-handled axe and the long, ready for the woods before tomorrow's light.

On Tuesday morning I'll wake and search the mountain air for the chainsaw's song; only rise when I hear it cry.

Substitute

OUR TEACHER, MR Noonan, is sick in the hospital. He might die. The substitute says we're to write him a letter.

Picturing his white eyebrows looking at the hospital ceiling, I do more than that. I Sign my name; give away a piece of my life to make him feel better.

The pain is so much worse than I remember, I have to grip my desk with my working hand. The frozen one dropped the pen. I stuck my foot out to stop it clattering, but I know the other girls are looking. One lung is a stone and I know my face is bright red like Lissie Ryan when she got her period years early and was afraid to move or say anything. I taste blood.

The blue-black grooves in the desk wood swirl. They were words, shapes, names. The girls who made them are long gone, children grown to adults, girls grown to mothers. But I know I'll never move.

The substitute comes round to pick up our letters. Her lips go thin when she sees the page with only my name on it but I'm just relieved. She might have made us bring them to the top of the class.

I have to take the school bus home, not ride my bike. Because I feel sick, it's easier to ignore the whispers and digs from those that saw what the substitute didn't.

A month later, Mr Noonan came out of hospital, but he never came back to school. When I saw him on the street one day, he thanked me for the letter I wrote, like I was just one of the others.

Loud

MY FATHER DOESN'T shout, but his voice hurts my head. In school we learned that loudness is different to volume. Loudness is how it feels to you.

The Weather Cycle

WINTER-RAINED SUN POLISHES the road to a pitch mirror. If the flash of yellow at my feet is my bike, I must be the dark shape above. The grass by the side of the road is a green I've never seen outside a film.

I pedal hard enough to sweat while the shower prickles my skin cool. I could cycle like this forever.

Instead of going home, I glide past people, watching how they are in the rain. Some act as if they don't notice or care. Others cover their hair with one hand and run between shop doors and awnings, cars and the poor shelter of bare trees.

The woman from the pub hunches her shoulders under the lumpy paint of the narrow door arch, making herself a smaller target for the rain. She lights her cigarette. Does my father taste death from her mouth when he—I skid and the wet hiss of my tyres bark, throw dirt up my leg.

Enda finishes her cigarette and watches a tiny river take the butt to the drain.

I don't notice the rain stop until drops from my fringe

tickle my face. My clothes cling to me. I shiver in the sun, even though I was warm in the rain.

Everything looks cleaner, but it's not. None of it.

When I look past her, beyond the church and the graveyard, there's a rainbow over my house.

Of course there is, when I'm not there.

Family Photo

IN THEIR BEDROOM I find a photograph of my mother holding me as a baby. I'm looking up at her with a puzzled expression. My short fingers reach but can't quite touch her face. She's staring at the camera, or at the man who must be holding it, baffled as me.

If someone took a picture of me looking at this photograph, my expression would be the same, and I think hers is too.

Biology

WE SHARE BIOLOGY class with the Christian Brothers boys. The one next to me squirms in his seat, making a show of being paired with the weird girl, feigning a smell I'm only half sure isn't there.

I think he likes me, so I stare at the hard plastic lungs, kidneys, heart and spleen and wonder if my insides are like that; brightly coloured, dead.

Stained Glass

I'VE BEEN CYCLING past the pub, stopping, cycling past again, searching for proof of where my father is, if it's where they say he is when he leaves us at the weekend.

I jerk the front brakes when I hear him through the stained-glass window. Stagger to a stop.

I don't catch his words. They're wrapped in a laugh I've never heard; a wet broadcasting thing, lifting at the end to invite others in. Not the clipped, final-word-on-the-matter shutdown I know.

When I push hard to escape it, too furious to admit I'm jealous, the teeth of a pedal tears my shin.

Hitting Houses

THERE ARE HITTING houses where fathers hit mothers hit children hit brothers hit sisters. Kelly's is one, they say. And the Sarsfield boy gets hit and hits back. I heard it, cycling past on a brittle night, nearly loud enough to knock me off my bike.

Mine is not a hitting house.

There must be a time in those houses, a time that's quiet and tight. Before the shouting screaming throwing swearing kicking breaking hitting. When it builds builds builds then explodes. When the crackle and thunder rattles the walls, shakes the chimney, scatters the birds until…

Boom.

Then gone. The air clean crisp clear.

What if that storm never broke?

This. My house. That's what.

Dad's not one for shouting. He drinks, but not at home. Uses his hands, but not to hit. To grab grip hold; her, not me.

Instead an endless build up crushing with too much

pressure in too small a space. There's no room for it. No room for us and it.

I hold my breath. The house holds its breath.

We don't hit. We don't shout. We choke on motes of tension that hang in the air, visible only from certain angles, but coating everything.

When I check the sky for signs of violence, cycling home, I find it on the other side of the mountain, brewing ominous cloud.

The Stages of a Bruise

PINK ON MAM'S inner arm, darkening to red. That means less than a day. I looked it up.

Three days of cardigans and jumpers, even in the stifling kitchen. When she reaches up for the plates, I see it darker blue than the willow pattern. A halo the same purple as the eyeshadow I bought that she won't let me wear.

By the time she loses the long sleeves, it's pale green. A poor match for the cabbage she soaks to go with his bacon.

On his news program, they talk about deterrence. How it could be becomes how it is.

Has she forgotten it's there?

A week later Mam needs to get the bedsheets off the line before the evening dew, but she sits on the chair outside the kitchen window, catching the last weak square of yellow sun.

Through distorted glass, I watch her touch the faded brown and know she hasn't forgotten.

The slow stiff rise of her arm when she unpegs the white-again sheets says she thinks she's left it too late.

My Voodoo Movie

I WRITE MY father's name over and over on a scrap of paper while I watch him from my bedroom window, waiting for a stagger or fall as he walks across the yard. I had the idea while watching a film where a woman stuck pins in a doll.

Dad clenches and releases his hand but that means nothing. He often grabs at things not there.

My breath sings in my ears when he stops outside the shed where he cuts timber, sells it, delivers it to burn in other people's houses.

But he walks on, fading into the murk of the shed.

I've covered the paper in so much ink it sticks to my hand and only lets go with a tacky wet kiss.

I open the tin by my knee. I didn't want to use the matches with their traitorous smell, but I light one with a rasp, knowing I look like a black and white film star in its trembling light.

I touch it to the corner of the paper, then drop it in the tin.

My hand fights me, wanting to close the lid, but fire

needs air to breathe, enough to destroy itself in darkness.

When I seal the tin, I keep my palm against the metal, even though it burns. Because it burns, like failure.

After Dinner

MY FATHER TOUCHES his fingers in a steeple, his elbows either side of a dinner plate smeared with mint gravy, the fat of a lamb chop, a countable number of peas.

Above cutlery crossed in a low x, he dies.

Mam talks about a cow two fields down tangled in the fencing. She eats mostly with her fork, moving it in spirals above her food. Like a Yank, he'd say. She knows he won't answer, but doesn't realise this time is different.

My seat at the table faces my father and the window. The thick glass above him distorts the clouds, as if they detour around him.

I know he's dead. I can smell the smoke from the note I burned with his name on it. I'd wondered what life I could take from him, give to her, take for myself.

I could Sign my name now to save him or write it in gravy on my plate.

Mam is quiet. She looks from her plate to him, waits for the slow blink to end. When it doesn't, she looks to me. Her lips move, but I can't hear the question or maybe she can't form the words.

Clouds slide flat across the sky.

When Mam lays down her fork, she's careful to make no noise.

We sit in the silence, listening to how it's changed.

Book 2

My Year of Useless Miracles

January (2)

MAM RECOVERED FROM her marriage, but her body is sick. The hospital can do no more. I move the TV to her room, sit and watch it while she looks past the screen. After I've Signed a bit of my life to her I look past it too, waiting for the pain to ease.

Feb (2)

HER COUGH IS a smoker's cough, though she never smoked. I want to say she must have caught it from Dad, who must have caught it from the woman whose ashtray mouth he shared for all those years, but we don't talk about him.

The TV is always on, even with the sound off, but there's a program about petrified forests we both watch.

Mar (3)

I WAKE IN the chair by her side so often I pull my bed into her room.

Signing doesn't make her better, only stops her from getting worse. She can't talk. The one word she uses might be a cry, might be; 'Loveen.'

Apr (5)

FIVE IS THE most I've Signed in a month. My hand twitches when I reach for the pen, rebelling. When it's done, I shake under the blanket.

May (7)

MAM'S COUGHS ARE a well full of muddy water. She clings to the visiting nurse and prayers; but it's me, I'm the one keeping her alive.

June (11)

SOME DAYS IT'S hard to tell which one of us is sicker. I put a show on for the nurse, make sure to be near the door so I don't take all day to let her in.

July (5)

EACH ONE OF Mam's breaths has a whimper in it. As short as the last, or shorter.

August (6)

I'M READY FOR the ice up my arm, my lung to stiffen. Not ready for Mam's hand on mine.

I thought she didn't know; but she wants me to stop.

When I move the pen under her hand, there's no jolt and my hand stays warmer than hers. The light leaves the room and her eyes are two quarter moons, setting.

I hear her voice but can't see her lips.

September (—)

LOVEEN...

October (—)

LOVEEN...

November (—)

...

December (—)

—

How We Met

BRITTLE AIR RATTLES my lungs as I pedal the slow rise from the old cemetery. Mam's not in that one, she's in the valley plot, where the earth above her has settled.

Seeing the new houses, the school gates and the classrooms beyond for the last time is like seeing them for the first time.

My breath draws too fast and too deep, but I only need to get to the top of the hill. At the crest I see the traffic lights below are green. They'll change before I get there, so I straighten my legs and let gravity take care of it.

As I lean into the breeze, it sings the kind of tuneless hum my mother used to make as she drifted around the kitchen when Dad was alive.

The Cork Dublin road is one of the busiest in the country. Even a glancing kiss from the slowest car will send me spinning. When one hits me properly, there'll be no more humming, only silence.

When the lights turn red, I lift my arms, but what hits me isn't metal and toughened plastic. It's the skin, muscle and bone of a young man. He wraps me in a high tackle

that would have him sent off the rugby field, he jokes
later, after I find out his first name is Finn, like my last
name; but before I have our baby.

We Made A Baby

HIS BODY.

Mine.

The first time (for me).

He comes. The cold leak of it on my thigh. I don't.

To not look at it, to look at something else but not look away, I put my hand on his hip. Jut. The word makes a shimmy in my stomach. The bone fits in my hollow palm.

What I don't know, amongst all I don't know, is that I am.

We are.

How I Told Him

FINN LEADS ME to the woods in a snowstorm. It sounds like the start of a murder story, but it's a date.

He's made sure I have the right coat and boots and there's chocolate and raisins in a backpack. I'm learning Finn likes to be near trees as much as my father liked to cut them down.

The forest is an outdoor room, blocking the storm, dulling the sounds. The wind plays lonesome songs on the higher branches. The trees shush it, then invite it back, let it grow again.

A bough creaks under the weight of snow. Our thick socked boots crunch through it.

The fingers of the storm curl through the trees and tug me forward to a clearing with the sky is white as the ground and snow flurries in fallen clouds.

I stop. Feel a snowflake melt on my cheek. I blink and know the lash is wet by its weight. My devastated lungs are huge and pink in my chest, celebrating each cleansing breath with a proof of life that hangs in front of me.

Finn is an outline on the other side of the clearing.

If I move, I'll lose the me standing in this moment.

He turns, looks at my face, then down to my hand on my belly.

When he looks up, he knows.

The Grip

FINN IS GOOD at doing the things my father did. I mustn't let that make me hate him.

It's our baby, but I'm the one who throws up. I use that to tell Finn why I'm sick, not just in the morning.

How I Signed pieces of my life away.

How I saved my dog, then let him die.

How I kept my mother alive until she wouldn't let me trade my life for hers, in the end.

How I let my father die at the kitchen table. A massive heart attack; they said. If he had a massive heart he kept it secret, I say, but Finn doesn't laugh.

I tell him I don't know if I have enough life left for the baby. That I gave it away before I knew what it was worth.

Finn doesn't believe me, of course. Otherwise I couldn't have told him. When I tell him that people around me die, he shakes his head and holds me, tells me that's enough of all that.

Finn holds an axe the same way as my father did and I have to I remind myself there are only so many ways to hold an axe.

Portrait

'CELIA, DO YOU hear it, the music?'

I remember the tilt of my mother's head, the stillness across her shoulders when she asked. She wanted to know if I could hear the tunes she found around the house. The ones she said her mother sang, ingrained in the walls and windows. I told her I could, and she smiled because she knew I was lying.

I'm so tired from the baby I forget how Mam looked, but I have the urge to draw her from before she got sick. When I hold the pencil over the paper I see cups clear from the table, plates stack in the dresser, forks drop between knives and spoons, each in their beds, all by her hand. Such long fingers. She played tin whistle one day when I brought one home from the nuns, but never played it again, no matter how often I asked.

I see her in outline, bones and elbows in a long shapeless dress. There's a glimpse of her, arms raised in the faraway windstorm of a sheet thrown over a bed as she made it. The nod of her head to the singing birds while she hung my father's clothes to dry before Friday night, when he'd leave the house without her.

I hear the shh of the hard brush across the floor, a minor storm ahead of her soft step. The water in the sink, the click of her wedding ring against a pan. It's the ghost of them all that pricks tears, but not what blinds me. That's the absence of her now. And then.

Later I'll sing to my baby. It soothes one of us, sometimes both. I don't know the songs either, so I drift between them all until the grandchild Mam never met falls asleep.

I hear it, Mam, the music. I hear the air between humming and singing that made you less lonely. I hear it, but always in another room.

I write her name in the corner of the blank page, knowing I've caught a good likeness.

Sunday Drive

THE BODY OF the car makes small dying sounds, but we're silenced by what went before. Black ice, I hear later, from someone who wasn't there.

I wasn't there all the time either, slipping in and out of consciousness.

I remember we tilted. Finn kept his feet on the pedals, tried to steer into it, but the wheels had already left the road by a tiny fatal measure.

The car contorted in outraged angles as we flipped more than once into the steep-sided valley. The short outbreak of violence slammed my knee against the glove compartment which vomited coins, sunglasses, Silvermints, a tape, pens, one glove, bills paid and unpaid.

In the rear-view mirror, twisted foolishly to the passenger side, I see Billy's small perfect hands but not his face as he sits strapped in his little throne.

I call his name but it's Finn who makes a small wet sound. There's blood in the crunched glass halo of the side window around his head.

I twist to see Billy properly, calling him, begging him

to make a sound, to cry. We'd taken the drive to soothe him after a long and wailing night and now that's all I want to hear.

My good little boy rewards me with a solitary moan and I reach back to him. The movement unlocks my seatbelt and in this tilted new gravity I drop on to Finn, crushing him. As I scramble to climb off him, to stop killing him, the only grip my fingers find is on a pen.

Later, I make the person who wasn't there tell me again about the twisted strap from the baby car seat across the throat.

But when she asks me about the writing on the back of my hand, I turn away. Stare out the hospital window.

Clarity

WHEN I'D TOLD Finn I could Sign parts of my life away to someone else, he didn't believe me, but still made me agree; never again.

Now I'm in St Joseph's, with its wet looking green paint, sitting by Finn's bed, waiting for him to wake.

My wheelchair creaks. The nurses say I should use it while I'm weak. How wise these women, no older than me.

A man two beds down the ward looks at me, looks through me, looks away.

Finn's eyes open, pick me out of the strange surroundings. When he smiles, it tugs something inside him, makes him wince. He tries to lift his hand but can't, so I slide mine under.

'Billy?' Finn's voice is so scratched a nurse brings water in a glass with a built-in straw. Finn stares at me through every painful swallow.

A doctor speaks, and I am stunned by the certainty of her words when she explains the awful thing. She's calm, clear, sympathetic. Finn examines me through every word and I feel his thumb move across the scrubbed raw welts on the back of my hand.

Billy and Finn took the worst of the crash, the doctor says, then pauses. Makes a space, so when she tells him our son is dead, there's no confusion, no hope.

I'm Not

WHEN I LEAVE the hospital, I'm no one's mother.
    At home, I'm no one's daughter.
    At night in our bed, I'm no one's at all.

How I Talk About My Child, Who Died

Not Every Sinner Wants Redemption

THE MAN I love returns to our childless house.

I refuse to let him in.

Refuse to be forgiven.

Close the door between us.

I listen as he picks up the bags I packed for him. Listen as he walks away. Listen when he's long gone.

Things I Know About The Dead

I WAKE TO the sound of pipes at a funeral. It can't be anyone I know, because everyone I know is dead or gone.

It's time to make a bonfire. Strip paintings from the walls, empty drawers and the content of wardrobes onto a pyre. To remember what I know about the dead. There are spaces at my table. A queer phrase of Mam's will never surprise again. There's no puzzle now in Dad's silence. They've done all they'll ever do.

What wakes me in the night won't be my baby's cry. My arms ache when I hold them in certain ways; crooked and small in front of me, or raised apart the width of a man's shoulders when I change the sheets on a double bed, pillows smooth on one side. These are things I know.

I WATCH A shower cross the valley. The weather you see is usually the weather you're in but this is a thing apart. A house of rain with a cloud roof tumbling through the fields. Ahead of it the wilful sun picks out a barn with a yellow roof.

I imagine the rain drops on the barn, light at first, tapping like pebbles, then heavier, building to a rumble loud enough that the cattle look up from machines that keep sucking milk for absent calves.

It must be two miles away, but I shiver.

The bottle of Jameson I bought to feel what my father felt makes a setting golden sun above the mountain while I pour it on the last logs he cut. Every swig I took made me retch.

The shower moves on. The yellow roof emerges, gleaming more than ever while the concrete walls, reluctant to release water, stay dark. I wait for that cleansing shower to reach me but it becalms in the valley, fading into the lesser day.

I drop a match on the scraps of paper and photos, all their clothes. It catches so quickly. Two lifetimes, three, with not even a whoosh. The smoke scalds my lungs and I take a deeper breath to silence questions I can't ask or answer.

In the morning I'll hear pipes again, this time through ash-stained glass and smoke-stained curtains in a silent house.

My mother's face melts in a photo's curl and I know I've made another mistake. I add that thought to the fire, feeling the heat of it crust the tears on my cheeks.

Book 3

One Foot in My Grave

A MAN COMES to my door. Not the man I waited for.

I tell him that, but he puts his foot in the doorway when I try to close it.

'I need to talk to you.'

'I've nothing worth stealing. Move your foot.'

'I'm not here to steal.'

'And you'd tell me if you were? Move your foot.'

'I need to talk to you about—'

'Jesus? Are you here to talk about Jesus? He's not in. If it's about life insurance, you're wasting your time. If it's charity, I've already given. Move your—'

He holds up a cracked plastic pen and writes in the cold air. Tells me he knows what I can do.

'I'm sorry,' he says, both feet now inside. Not sorry enough to leave me be.

He walks past me, into my house, and I feel what men must feel in front of bigger men with more violence creased in their skin. What women feel so many days. What my mother felt in this house, this room.

Helpless.

I Know What You Can Do

'I KNOW WHAT you can do. I heard your father talk about it.'

When the stranger speaks, rough weather erupts in my kitchen. Gales rip away chunks of his voice and the things I hear make no sense. I catch that he was a barman in Casey's, where Dad practically lived on weekends. I'm mentioned.

The biro on the table between us doesn't stir so, nor a hair on his head, so the storm may be localised. I grip the table, just in case.

'With her?' I ask, to stop him talking.

'Who?'

'Enda. My father, with Enda.'

He laughs. 'I don't think so.' Then, 'No, not like that.' Sometimes, when someone says something, it's true.

I don't know if the storm is dying or if I'm in its eye but I have a moment to think.

So Dad's affair was with the bottle. Not a woman. That changes everything. Changes nothing.

The sound of far off thunder is the man talking about

his daughter. How sick she is.

My mind is working on whether my father made his deal with himself or with my mother; to live sober all week in return for drink at the weekend? I know he didn't make it with me. I got a space where a father should be. Wound so tight in terror of a slip, he infected us all. A man who told the pub how proud he is of his daughter; and never told her.

This man in front of me loves his daughter, and I'm sure she knows, but it's him the doctors have told to prepare for the end.

So he wants to make a deal, to ask a woman to make an impossible choice so he can have what he says he needs. He's hardly the first.

'I'm sorry your daughter is sick,' I say.

It's the kindest way I can tell him no, I won't be that sacrifice.

Drowning Hazards in the Traditional Irish Kitchen

IT'S MORE THAN a minute since I last took a breath.

The man's begging pushed me from my chair but when I tried to stand I found my kitchen floor was made of water.

Now its bright reflection dances on the ceiling above me while I sink. The man leans over me. He sees I can't breathe, but doesn't know what to do.

He'd dropped by to ask a small favour, a Sunday morning kind of thing. Only give away a chunk of my life for his dying daughter, since he'd heard in a pub I had a bit of the witch in me.

I try to make him see the oxygen tank by the fridge by glaring at it, by cupping my hand over my mouth. He grows smaller but I can't tell if I'm falling or he's moving away.

A silver flash like a turning shoal tells me he's found the tank. I lose him in the reef of chair and table legs and float closer to the seabed.

The underwater chime of the oxygen tank by my head opens my eyes and the man with the sick daughter unrolls the tube, cups the mask, then hesitates.

It lasts less than a second, but we both see it.

His dark halo. Negotiation.

When he clamps the mask to my face, I push his hand from it and twist the valve so the hiss of oxygen hangs between us like a curse.

He's had my answer more than once today and when I break the surface, when I can breathe my own breaths, I'll tell him again.

Negotiations

'I LET MY father die in that chair,' I tell him. 'Didn't pick up a pen to save him.'

His instinct to stand is beaten by his talked-out exhaustion.

This man knew my father better than I did. Knew a man who talked loud in pubs, told jokes. Heard him sing, heard him talk about me like I never did; with pride. Drunken pride, but I would have taken that.

I knew a man who said no. Or nothing at all. Who'd choke a conversation. Say, "Ah, we're getting into territory there." Now I know he was terrified the wrong word would pull out the log that held the stack in place.

'I tried to save Mam until she couldn't bear to see it and made me let her go.'

He looks at the bare walls, at the pen on the table, at me, but I know all he sees is his daughter. We're united and opposed in our beliefs. He believes I could save the girl. I believe that would kill me.

It's not like I don't understand his agony.

'My son....' Oh I understand his agony, 'I didn't do

this thing for him, that you want me to do for your daughter.'

One face of the biro shines on the table between us. When he picks it up it disappears in his fist.

'That was Finn Ryan's boy?'

My face must tell him how grave his error is.

'It's a small town,' he says.

Negotiations happen in the silences.

'It's time for you to go.'

I wait till he hits me or walks away.

The blank sky behind him twists in the old kitchen window glass.

He slams the biro back on the table. White veins in the plastic.

Dad's chair scuttles when he stands. It teeters on one leg, and in the time it takes him to stride to my front door, falls. He'd bet everything on me, and lost.

When the car door has slammed, the tyres have thrown gravel and the engine growled down the valley I go to the door. I cling to the spot where paint can't hide the grain. Now he's gone I have no one to ask anything at all.

If my cursed gift is real, I could have helped his daughter. If it's not, there's nothing I can do.

And nothing I could have done to save my baby, even if I'd tried.

Homemade Weather

I STAND BY my front door for long minutes because when I move my feet, they sink in damp green moss. An impossible carpet on a floor that never had one. There are freshwater freckles on my shoes from the mountain stream that runs down a stairs that was plain wood this morning. My skin prickles with the change of air around water, cooler, cleaner, bright. This is not a leaking pipe or an overflowing bath, this is a small river.

On the landing uncut hay sways in the same breeze as the lampshade. The back window glows with summer sun on a winter day.

Nested in the smells of the meadow are the sounds of my grandfather calling and the chuckle of an old tractor engine. The shadows on the back wall are of haycocks and pitchforks and times before my time.

When I turn to the kitchen, frost decorates the sink and taps, draws spirals on the jug of water. Ice crisps the folds of a teatowel.

The seat of my chair is a windblown forest and there are clouds above the kitchen table. They churn grey over the old oak, moving across the wood plain, raining on the dent valleys, rising above the knot mountains. The cups and plates contain what they can but already overflow, freeing small waterfalls to the floor.

I know I can't be here anymore, at the mercy of homemade weather.

Caoineadh

I WALKED FROM the house where I've hidden for decades. Left the door open, but I don't know if I'm going back.

The short trek to the mountain woods took all my breath. The branches trap my keening while I sit and wait for it to return to me. I hear my mother's noise in it, her grieving the lives she hadn't lived.

Once they paid women to weep and wail at funerals, to lament. The women in my house paid to do it. Me with my baby, my mother with her silence.

I've come to the mountain like my childhood dog Ollie, the last time he got sick. He wanted to be out of sight, at the end. I watched him and let him go. When I searched for him later, there was no sign.

Through the trees I see a clearing like one where I was breathless as this, a lifetime ago. We'd walked in snow, Finn and me. That day I was afraid to move past a perfect moment when I knew I was alive, and there was a life in me, in case it shattered.

But I did.

And it did.

Catch Me When I Fall

FROM A TREE stump across the valley, I see a car pull up outside the house where I spent my life, the house I fled today.

Though I'd told him not to, the father of a dying girl has come back, as I suppose I knew he would. He walks through the open door, expecting to see me, expecting a miracle, but he'll find neither.

Thirty-four years ago my mother brought my precious weight through that door in her arms. Was there a smell of drink when she walked in, or had my father already made his arrangement? Dry through the week, yielding at the weekend.

Another shape emerges from the car, skinny legs and a jacket so big it must be her father's. My trigger finger jolts on the cracked pen in my pocket.

She examines the house. Looks up at my bedroom window, cataracted by weak sun. Ellie he called her. She puts her arms out and turns with one toe pointing to the sky. A slow pirouette for a child who wants to play but doesn't have the strength.

At the end of her spin she bows to the car. No, not to the car. To someone inside it.

The car door opens and I know who it is before I know who it is. I stand and make a noise too weak to be heard across the fields but the movement is enough to draw the girl's eyes. She points and the man turns and my skin itches on the back of my hand where I once Signed for him. Finn.

The desperate father has played all his cards at once. But maybe outsmarted himself. He's left me with a choice. If I walk down the mountain, I won't have the strength to Sign anything. If I Sign anything, I won't have the strength to walk down the mountain.

Finn is running.

Finn is running away from the house we shared for so few years.

Finn is running to me. Across the yard. Across the road. Into the valley before the climb. I lose sight of him in the dip and look at the girl. Sick and scared like I was so often. But she has her father's hand tender on her shoulder.

I take the pen from my pocket, paper from another, afraid of what I'm going to do, terrified by what I might not.

I Sign my name.

Cold rushes up my arm and into my chest, squeezing the breath from me. I drop the pen and though I fight it, my eyes close before Finn emerges from the valley.

As I sway, with the mountain at my back, I have the strongest feeling he'll catch me when I fall.

What The Fox Brings In Its Jaw

Ian O'Brien

What The Fox Brings In Its Jaw

ANOTHER CRAVING HAS brought him to the window and he is standing there with a cigarette when he sees it. The window is open, he's not supposed to be smoking, and he doesn't want to risk another complaint. The cigarette burns down to his fingertips, and he isn't really looking at anything, perhaps the row of lights in the distance, beyond the pylon-lined blackness, when he sees the fox move into the rectangle of light below. His eyes follow it and he holds his breath. It stops for a moment, as if sensing him, standing up there on the third floor, silhouetted in the kitchen light. It holds something in its jaw. At first he thinks it's a rat or a vole, something drooping down but when its shape loosens, fans out, he realises it's a bird, a blackbird maybe or a magpie. It's almost too big for the fox to hold and it lets it go for a second to readjust, snapping it back up tightly but, he senses, gently. It begins to move off again, silently back into the dark, through the bins and the flats beyond towards the black expanse of fields, its prey held tight, precious. He watches it go, aware his heart is racing, and he breathes again.

When she was small they had watched for foxes in the woods. He had taken her down, at dawn, wrapped her up in gloves and a coat too big, and they had crouched in whispers by the old bridge near the farmhouse, watched them dart across the pathway, from field into bracken, nettles, streaks of fox-shape against the pale light. She had squealed and tightened her grip on his hand. Her mother had protested at first but turned over in the bed, heavy with sleep, glad to have the house and the end of the night to herself. His own father had taken him to the same spot years before and they had watched badgers come within yards of them.

He closes the window and washes his hands. They are red and raw and there is a clumsy prison tattoo by his thumb, the start of a cross.

He stops the tap and looks again into the dark. The fox has gone. His eyes lift to the constellation of lights that line the distance, that mark the next town over, and he thinks of her, sleeping. He wonders if her mother kept up the lie, the job on the oil rigs, far out at sea. He still has her letters folded in a cigarette tin. How it made him feel when her drawings reached him. He wonders if she still remembers, still thinks of him, her hand in his as the fox crosses their path.

Tracks

HE MOVES THROUGH the woods like a ghost. His hands are stuffed into thin pockets and his breath makes shapes in the mist. Beneath his feet the crunch of snow sounds hollow, false, as if the sound is trapped, reduced and for a second he thinks he can hear his own heart beating. There are tracks in the snow and he follows them. Tiny, certain pads. It is getting light but not quite and the snow holds its own glow, like trapped moonlight. He doesn't stop when he sees the drops of blood, he is almost expecting this. Though for a second he thinks it might be his own and he checks his arm, pulls at his loose sleeve and is relieved to find it dry. That had happened once before, in a pharmacy. He had stood there, a zombie, frozen in place in the aisle and a girl had said 'Mummy, he's bleeding.' He had looked down and there had been a drop, drop, drop on the floor, and he had tracked the thin line up his finger, through the palm, the wrist and up the bony length of arm to the wasteland of the inner elbow. The mother had taken the daughter away, whispered not to look. He had felt something like dull horror trapped behind glass, a clouded scream somewhere inside the brain. Life in the veins, he'd thought, and had smiled.

His coat is too big and the silhouette he makes against the snow is like a scarecrow. Shoulders like gallows. He feels the wind blow through him like scaffolding, the way it did before when he still worked on the roofs. Before the site manager had took him aside in the pub, had a quiet word, pushed a stuffed envelope into his hand and wished him luck, said he had a kid of his own, would kill him if he ever touched the stuff. A look that said his sympathy was culled.

The spots are only small and have dropped between the prints. Fox, he thinks. And when he sees feathers he wonders if it had been quick for whatever it had caught. A snap of the neck, a click of the jaw and away through the snow, its eyes closed, carried.

Soon he will reach a clearing, and he will make his own tracks across, the town coming to life in the distance. The fields will drop to dirt-track and twist into streets and he will wind his way through the industrial estate and down to the high street. He will find his usual spot, a space between two shuttered shops and unroll the sleeping bag strapped across his back. He will hold out a sign that will lie that he is clean, the paper cup steadied with a handful of coins.

The tip of his thumb will feel for the wedding ring, long pawned. In the woods, a blackbird calls to its young unheard.

Ghosts

He whispers to her, they have to be still and silent. They have waited for what has felt like hours and she's grown afraid and has started to cry. Not real tears but she wants to go home, wants Mummy, her bedroom. The forest is heavy with silence and mist. Just another minute, he lies, and an owl hooting somewhere makes her cry for real.

Her mother had protested at first, had snapped down the light and squinted, asked what the hell he was playing at. He was still drunk, she said. 'It's five o'clock in the bloody morning.' He had been reminiscing, putting on records long into the night and dredging over the past. And every time he came at last to the moment his own dad had taken him to the woods at dawn to watch for foxes. 'I'll take her too, one day,' he'd said, though she never thought he would actually do it.

'She's too young,' she said, 'it's freezing.'

'I'll put an extra coat on, and gloves,' he said, though she had already turned over and snapped the lamp switch off, pulled the blanket tight around her and huddled into a defiant silence.

'I'll be careful,' he said. And then stronger, almost aggrieved, 'she's my daughter too.' His head still swam with booze and he dressed clumsily in the dark.

'You're cracked,' she said.

HE HAD WOKEN her gently and she'd looked puzzled as he pulled her clothes on over her pyjamas, struggled with the boots. She'd asked for her Mummy as he pulled gloves onto her hands that were too big. 'Like playing ghosts,' he'd said, 'we have to be quiet.'

The streets were silent and dark, the windows curtained, blank. The cold had sobered him up and he wondered if he was doing the right thing. She walked without speaking at his side, her boots loud. The black woods loomed into view.

'I want to go back,' she said, and he stopped to pick her up and she dozed against his shoulder.

It was true that his own father had brought him when he was young, the same spot by the old farmhouse bridge. They had watched badgers come within yards of them once. Over years the memory had become enshrined, added to, magic almost. Even after they had stopped speaking, after the trouble, he remembered it with a kind of detached pride. Crouching in the shadows as the badgers fired past, hunting. An electric excitement that would bind them forever. Only now, as his own daughter's fingers pulled at his, he remembered that he hadn't been excited at all, he had been afraid. His dad had been disappointed, he felt it on his shoulders all the way home.

'Let's go home,' he says, only it is then that they see it.

It darts across the pathway, from field into bracken, into nettles, a streak of fox-shape against the pale light. She squeals and tightens her grip on his hand, electric.

The Grey Men

THE DAWN IS stillborn, promising only cold. There is
sleet forecast but for now yesterday's snow is stubbornly
in place. A dog has pissed in his usual spot in the space
between the shuttered shops and it has frozen into black
ice. He finds half a newspaper and he puts this down on
top of the black patch, then puts the sleeping bag down
on top of it. He settles in for the day. The cold makes his
breath like ghosts.

There is a thaw, almost, or a dazed awakening and the
city starts to disconnect from the night. It's in limbo, the
buildings seem to dig into the dark against the police-blue
sky. Cranes move, lift their anchors from the thinning
dark and the city moves, slow. A bus somewhere and a
shutter coming up and a bin-lorry backs up into an
alleyway, bleeping like an alarm-clock. He puts the paper
cup down and blows on his fingers. A coin drops into it.
It is Ahmad, passing to the other side of the square to set
up. He says something in Arabic, the same each morning,
and he never asks what it means, just half raises his hand
as he passes. Ahmad is already painted grey and he

imagines him painting his face in the harsh light of a bathroom, venturing out into the black morning, moving across the city, a spectre. He wonders if anyone sees him, if he has to take a bus, imagines the driver too long in the job to raise an eyebrow. Ahmad puts a wooden box down that he has carried across the city and he wraps himself in a sheet that he has unbundled. The first commuters are arriving, heads down, hands stuffed into pockets as if holding down the change. Occasionally there is a tinkling in the suitcase that Ahmad has opened out on the ground and he bows like a mannequin, a shop mannequin come to life.

The nearest shutter comes up and the shopkeeper steps out, the mortuary-white light behind him lancing the black pavement. He walks across and reaches down, offers him a cigarette, as he always does.

'Good luck,' he says, as he always does. He returns to the shop, pulls up a second shutter like an eye.

The stream of commuters thickens and a woman stops by and places a cup of tea in a paper cup by him, smiles. She has done this twice now. He wants to say 'thank you' but the words are frozen in his throat and he nods. She walks on and his eyes follow her. She passes Ahmad who remains frozen in place and she doesn't look up. He can still smell her perfume, just, and he closes his eyes. The tip of his thumb stretches across the inside of his palm and he feels for the wedding ring.

Threads

SHE WROTE, AT the start. He kept the letters folded in a cigarette tin. First day at school, a photograph that he couldn't look at. She wove a story for their daughter; Daddy was working away on the oil rigs, like her own father had. To her he was helicopters, steel, sea, men in overalls you see on TV. Sometimes, as the rain lashed the window, she would wake afraid and imagine him at a window looking out, the wild sea raging beneath him, a hand pressed to the glass and she would lift her own hand to her bedroom window and watch the heavy drops on the other side, feel for them through the glass.

It had started, as always, with little things. Shoplifting. Toiletries to sell in the pub, tools from a hardware shop, a gold chain once. And then he'd met Anthony and they'd grown into warehouses, filling vans with stolen goods, serious. A reputation too big like an ill-fitting coat, hanging from his shoulders. She had threatened to leave him if he carried on, it was no way to raise a baby. But the final demand letters kept her threats at a distance, hollow. Every job was the last job. He was looking for work, was taken on as an apprentice roofer at one point but was let go. Reputations. He hawked building sites, shadow-eyed. A week here, a few days there, but nothing solid, dependable. Her parents disowned her eventually, and some nights he would wake in the dark and hear her crying.

The last job was a warehouse on the industrial estate. Too close to home he'd said but Anthony had talked him into it. Not on your own doorstep, his Dad had said, but it wasn't as if they were doing houses, never homes. He held onto that like a thread in the dark. It had been straightforward enough, a tip off from a security guard they knew and a gap between shifts. But the second guard had come on early and disturbed them. He said in court he didn't know about the knife, but that was only half true. Anthony had pulled it out in a panic and had pushed the guard against a wall, sirens going, a dog barking and suddenly tugging at him, making him wild. Himself shouting, running, a rabbit in the headlights. The guard appeared in court, a ruined man, bared his scar for the jury like a freakshow. Gasps. The judge catching his eye.

Once, she drew him. A small figure scrawled onto paper and cut out. She sellotaped a thread of cotton to him and opened the window into the wild night. She let him go, like a kite, held the cotton tight. The wind caught him and spun him, she watched him whirl against the dark. After a while she brought him back in, placed him on the radiator, waited for him to dry so she could try again to draw his face.

Red In The Snow

NEW YEAR'S EVE, not long after midnight, last orders. He was coming away from the bar with three pints spilling, a bag of nuts in his teeth. She was rummaging in her handbag for her emergency tenner and caught his elbow. The pint dropped and miraculously didn't smash, though its contents sloshed up and out and down his pants. There was an eruption of jeers from the rest of the queue and she held her hands to her mouth, apologising, and something in the way he stood with the nuts in his teeth staring after his lost pint made her laugh and she couldn't stop. She bought him a drink, he ordered two more. 'Make that four.' And that was that.

Coming outside, the world started to spin. She was hoarse from speaking and laughing and she held onto him like she was steering a gondola. It had started to snow and he lurched his head back, letting the flakes fall on his face and she laughed. 'You're cracked,' she said, and tightened her hold on his arm.

The taxi queue was like a shipwreck shore, people sat on steps, kerbs, some singing, crying, some asleep. She shivered and he put his coat around her clumsily and she could smell his aftershave and cigarettes in the leather and it reminded her of the coat her Dad wore when she was small. Home late from the pub on Fridays, her mother would send her to bed and the arguments would begin, and once he came upstairs afterwards, the coat still on, stood in her doorway, leaned in like a tilted scarecrow and she could smell the drink on him. He said he was going to leave, for real this time, was saying goodbye, and she half-believed him. He kissed her and the stubble on his chin as he missed felt like sandpaper. He had been crying. She was almost asleep when she heard the door slam. And the next morning, when she followed his footsteps in the snow to the end of the road there had been red drops by the lamppost. She had told her Mum and she had carried on folding his things, the rustle of the bin liner strong and taut.

She nestled into the coat. A fight was breaking out somewhere in the queue and he raised his voice to it, slurred, but she pulled him closer to her. 'Leave it,' she said. But the men who were fighting sought the distraction, welcomed it, and dragged him in. He was in no fit state, staggered like a punchdrunk boxer and it was over in seconds, one of the men following his girlfriend who had shouted and climbed into a cab, pulling him in. She helped him to his feet from the kerb where he nursed his lip.

'If you're gonna marry me you can pack that in,' she said, trying to laugh and finding she was serious, ridiculous. And when he kissed her she tasted blood.

Manslaughter Is Muddy Water You Cannot Wash Your Hands With

HE LOOSENS HIS jaw and the strap becomes slack and the needle is still in as his head hits the pillow and he's back

and now its grass and she's with him and she is holding a buttercup under his chin and the light it gives is everything

and the sun is on his skin but the thought is coming back like a black cloud and he's back,

back in the van and he is driving too fast and he's shouting at Anthony who still has the blade in his hand in the passenger seat. There is blood on it, *what did you DO?* Though he knows. A botched job. It was supposed to be easy, a gap in the security shifts, but the warehouse was filled with sirens, sirens, dogs barking, the guard shouldn't have been there

// the pillow is liquid, he is sinking into its inky black, warm as blood //

and he is back in the van and screeching off and he pulls at the wheel and there are girls on the corner beneath the streetlamp that has just come on and one girl is spinning, round and round the lamppost she goes, round and round, and he is looking at the knife, the blood on the knife and Anthony is shouting

look out

LOOK OUT

and he is back in the courtroom and there is a sobbing behind him and he knows her father is there, a man he knows and cannot bear to look at

and the mother has taken the stand

and there is a collective intake of breath in the gallery when she describes the moment she had seen from her window the van mount the kerb and how the sound it made as it hit her girl will stay with her forever.

Anthony had told him to drive on. And he had at first but reversed when he got to the corner. He had climbed out and pushed his way through the circle that had gathered around her. Anthony had climbed into the driver's seat and the van had screeched off into the dark. He knelt and took her head in his hands, cradled it, and the blood spread warm between his fingers.

He can still hear their voices. The fear and the panic in them, a wild baying from the younger ones. And the mother coming running, pulling at him, pulling him away from her, cradling her. A cry at first and then a disbelief, a stammering and then a hushing. Blue lights and compassionate voices. 'Time to let go.' A raw howling. It's in his bones now like calcium, recorded, trapped.

He loosens the strap and holds his arm like a broken bird on the bed, cradles.

Manslaughter is dirty water you cannot wash your hands with. A line from a letter, published in the local paper.

Blood has spread in the crease of his arm and it dries the shape of a buttercup.

His Things

SHE LEFT THEM to it, came outside for some fresh air. The room was hot and the light that forced through the drawn curtains made everything in the room red. The aunts were smoking. It filled the air like cobweb. 'You should have done this years ago,' they said. Her mum listened and half-smiled but it was a thin smile and though she nodded the eyes told a different story. 'You want to get this lot on a car boot,' one said, pulling a leather jacket from one of the bags and holding it up to the red square of the window. Her Mum had closed the curtains when a neighbour had looked in. 'Nosy bastards,' she'd said, and pulled the curtains to. 'You don't owe him anything,' her other aunt said.

She went outside to the shed, pulled the door closed behind her. She breathed deep and savoured it, the damp and the dust and the spiders and the stillness. When she was younger he would tell her that monsters lived in here, to keep from touching his tools. Most of it had been cleared out and sold or given away. She remembered a man in a vest coming to the house after seeing an ad in the paper and he had taken away boxes, and when he handed over the money he had whispered something and winked and she had seen. It made her feel sick and hot and she had come to the shed and kicked at what was left, punched at the wooden walls until her knuckles showed blood. Her Mum had come out and taken her inside, bathed her hand, silent. 'He's gone,' she'd said at last, and she didn't know if she meant the man in the vest or her Dad.

She could hear her aunt's voices. 'About time,' they were saying. 'Just like his father. The apple doesn't fall far from the tree.'

There was still a pair of his old work boots left, hanging on a nail like boxing gloves. She took them down and held them, sailed a thumb across the leather. She took off her own shoes and pulled them on, they came almost halfway up her shins, the laces loose and she could nearly picture him again. Her Mum called her in. 'Come and say goodbye,' she said. She came out of the shed and her Mum was stood at the backdoor. 'Take them off,' she said, though she wasn't angry, and she turned and went back into the house. An aeroplane passed overhead. There was a beer can and she kicked it. The tongue gripped tight, a sudden wrap that gave almost a gasp or a laugh.

The Places We Go When
The Wind Blows Cold

HE READ SOMEWHERE that when trees prepare for the winter, they drain the leaves of their nutrients, store them in their roots. Chlorophyl is one of the first to be broken down and it is this that gives leaves their green. Did he read it or did he see it on TV? Or was it something he learned at school? He thinks back to the dead-eye look his science teacher had and smiles. 'You never listen,' he'd said and he was right. Heard, never listened. Though there was a flash of something at school, something like electricity in the blood, brief as it was, alive against the grey. He looks down at his fingers, the tips have turned blue. Chlorophyl, he thinks, keeps the leaves green, the first to go, and he feels his bones ache like roots against the pavement.

The commuters have thinned in the lockdown. The woman who stops by every morning and places a cup of tea next to his sleeping bag has not been today. He imagines her at home, meetings online, the radiator on, watching the snow as it comes down. He should go back now. Back to the hostel, but he knows who will be there, waiting, has all eyes looking out for him, and he will not reason with him or anyone. Debts will be paid one way or another. Maybe he should just sleep here tonight.

It's like the world has stopped, the sun forgot to rise, the grey dawn cancelled. Even the planes have stopped, the birds reclaiming it in streaks of magpie, pigeon, crow. Sparrows make a beating ribcage of the bushes by the bus stop. He cannot feel his feet. Even Ahmad hasn't ventured out today. Ahmad, the Grey Man, who takes his spot on the corner of the square and stands and stands, never making a sound, moving a muscle, a ghost. Each morning for the past two weeks he has called on his way across the square, dropped a coin into his paper cup, said words in a language he doesn't understand. 'Good luck,' he says, 'God be with you.' And though he doesn't understand, he feels the words are kind, they glow, candles.

There is a space in the woods where he watched for foxes once and he thinks maybe he should go there, curl in with the foxes in the roots of an oak tree, sleep.

He is thinking of his family, elsewhere. They come to him like ghosts.

If Ahmad had called on his way across the square, dropped the coin into the cup, noticed he wasn't sitting up in his usual way, maybe he would have stopped. Maybe he would have called out to him, shook his shoulder, maybe he wouldn't; maybe he would have carried on to his own place on the corner, took to his box, the grey shroud covering him, waiting for the waves of commuters with their small change.

As gently as it started, the snow stops.

Five More Minutes

SHE CANNOT SEE the stars but they are there behind the snowcloud. Nobody is looking down from the hi-rise when the bottle rolls and smashes in the gutter. The laughs echo across the garages and their breaths make shapes in the cold. Her knuckles are still wet with blood where the tips have grazed but she won't go home to wash them clean because she doesn't want to have to stay in. Just five more minutes, then she will go and she will run upstairs and wash her hands and try not to scream, brush her teeth as quietly as possible to hide the smell of the booze and she will slink into the front room, catch the end of whatever show her Mum has fallen asleep to this time.

The knuckles happened an hour ago. One of the boys had emerged with a sledge, though the layer of snow was so thin that you could write your name in it and it'd go straight through to the tarmac below, not enough for a snowball, though they clawed at car bonnets all the same. Someone had stood outside the shop for almost an hour and eventually a man had given in and bought them a bottle of cider. And though she didn't feel drunk at all, she made a pantomime of falling around anyway and that's when someone emerged with the sledge. A cheap plastic thing that the handle had snapped on twice. They took it in turns dragging it around the carpark with one of them inside, most only lasting less than a minute before jumping out again, the feel of the tarmac racing beneath making the bones shake and the skin roar. She was the last to go and the plastic must have been as thin as the snow. Two boys pulled and the girls pushed and it took off across the frost dragging, a tormented roaring of tarmac and ripping plastic under the sulphur lights. She put her hands beneath her, not knowing that the plastic had just given way and when she did there was nothing between her skin and the speeding black but two millimetres of snow. It must have only been for a second but the pain was electric. She leaped off and shouted and kicked and swore and punched the air and they laughed and fell to the floor not seeing the flecks of red in the snow.

She should have gone home then. If she had, she could have bathed her hand, her Mum would have asked what had happened, bandaged it, sat her on the couch and laughed, talked, promised to be there more. She wouldn't have swung around the corner lamppost like the others, catching snow as it started to fall, wouldn't have been spinning arms wide, hand glistening as the speeding van mounted the kerb.

Close

'BUT WHAT IF it's him?'

'What if it isn't?'

The two of them stood by the shop doorway and looked down at the shape in the sleeping bag. He had his back to them, they could just about make out his head, a hat pulled down. He didn't make a sound.

'He could die out here. They do'. It was on the news.

They were whispering. The street was almost empty and it was trying to snow. She knelt down.

'Don't,' the boy whispered, eyeing the street.

She reached out her hand tentatively and then changed her mind, stood up.

'Let's go back, it's freezing,' he said.

'But we have to find him.'

'There are hundreds of them, we've no chance. Come on. We shouldn't have come.' He was afraid. The emptiness of the street made it worse. What if he woke up – dazed, angry, drunk, drugged? This was a mistake, he should never have agreed to come along.

'But what if it's him?' she whispered.

'It won't be.'

She had come out without a coat and regretted it. Her Mum had told her. Sat her down and told her everything. Wanted her to hear it from her instead of somebody else. He'd been spotted, a friend of a friend of someone in town, begging. And she had just run out the door, straight to her boyfriend's house. 'We have to find him,' she'd said, crying, and they had come out straightaway, ridiculous, like something in a film, the way you do at that age, impetuous, reckless, him shouting to his parents and banging the door behind him. It started to snow.

The figure in the bag was still as stone.

'If it was your Dad, you'd do the same. You'd want to find him.' Though she knew already that she wouldn't wake him. She wouldn't reach across and touch his shoulder. He wouldn't respond and turn and wake, wouldn't recognise her, wouldn't say her name.

She knelt back down and went as if to touch him and again she couldn't go through with it. She stood up.

'Come on,' he said, placing his own coat around her shoulders, the way they do.

Clean

IN HIS DREAM, it has rained during the night and the road through the woods shines gold in the morning sun. The last of the snow has washed away and taken with it the fox prints and the footsteps and the badger tracks. The road glistens, gilded. He shields his eyes as he walks and the hedges are alive again with birds. The trees are leafless, though in this light the wet branches shimmer silver. A raven sits high and preens, its feathers glossy, shining. It calls out and he feels it watching him, though not in fear.

Up ahead, he can make out the silhouette of his daughter. She is older now and she is waiting for him by the old farmhouse that they used to pass. Inside there will be a fire burning and no one will ask him to move along. He will dump his things, the rolled up sleeping bag and sit by the fire, take off his boots and hat and somewhere in the house will be the sound of children and they will be happy that he is in their front room dozing. They will draw pictures for him and when he wakes they will give them to him and he will recognise himself, drawn with a crooked smile. The dark circles will have gone and the hands will be open. They will draw him in colour.

She waits for him on the golden road, a silhouette, and as he walks towards her he fills his coat, his shoulders and back swell to meet the fabric like the sail of a ship blown full. They no longer hang from him, look borrowed. He will feel for the wedding ring with the tip of his thumb and it will be there again, look down and the prison tattoo removed, the hands clean and full.

He will reach her and she will open her hand to him.

Watching for Foxes

THE POLICE CAR moved alongside them, the engine ticking. The window came down on the passenger side and the officer put his head out slightly, though they couldn't really see his face.

'Where are you off at this time?'

They stopped and the car stopped too, though the engine kept ticking, a dull growl.

'Been watching for foxes,' the boy said and his dad put a hand on his shoulder, tight.

'Foxes?' He could sense he was looking at him, beyond the boy, reading him.

'That's right.'

'It's four in the morning. He should be in bed.'

'We're heading back now,' the man said and started to walk, the hand still tight on the boy's shoulder. The streets were dark and silent, the police car blazing, incongruous. The boy reached for his dad's hand and he took it, his hand hot.

'Just a minute,' and the officer opened the door, stepped out.

'What's in the bag?'

The man stopped and eyeballed the officer, who had pulled out a notebook. The driver was silent, though they could hear a voice on the radio.

'Nothing.'

'What's your name?'

'It's not illegal to take your son to the woods to look for foxes.'

'Name.'

He told him and pulled the boy closer to him.

The officer said something to the driver and there were more words from the radio. The boy's heart raced. The radio squealed again and the man lowered it.

'I'm going to need to take a look in the bag.'

MINUTES BEFORE, THE boy had emerged from the kitchen window of the farmhouse as silently as he had crept in. The woods were wild with eyes. His dad waited frantic, rigid, the bag ready. They walked in solid silence until they were at the bridge where they really had watched for foxes the time before, saw badgers within yards of them, hunting. He could tell from the boy's lowered head that he hadn't been successful.

'Well?'

'I couldn't reach it,' the boy said, and there was a fear there in the voice.

'I told you to use a chair.' The boy could tell that the anger was under the surface, like a river moving under ice.

'There was a noise. I think someone woke up,' he lied.

They walked through the woods in silence, nothing but darkness in the trees.

HE OPENED THE bag, relieved that the boy hadn't reached the carriage clock.

There was a moment of charged silence, interrupted only by the faint sound of the radio. The officer looked at the boy.

'Did you see any?'

'Any what?' the man answered, his hand returning to the boy's shoulder.

'Foxes,' the policeman said, and he looked from the boy to the man, held his eye.

'No,' the boy answered, and he looked to his dad. There was a long silence.

'Maybe next time,' the policeman said, and climbed back into the car.

Somewhere in the woods, a fox held a bird in its jaw.

The Impossibility of Wings

Donna L Greenwood

In The Night They Will Come For Me

THE HYENAS CAME for my mother when I was ten years old. They took her in the middle of the night and gobbled up her eyes. When they dragged her carcass back the next morning, her dark, empty sockets swallowed up our lives.

On Mum's good days, we watched her fly above the earth and bounce around the planets. My sisters and I were never able join her for we were tethered by the ropes of reality. All we could do was watch her play with the moon and hope that she would find her way home.

On other days – the black days – she would lie at the bottom of the ocean, staring at unfathomable things with her black-hole eyes. The silence of her depths terrified us.

'Mummy,' we cried, 'Mummy, swim upwards towards the light!'

But our mouths just filled with water and she let us drown a thousand times.

The intensity of her light spilled through the holes in her mind, blinding us all. We tried so hard to plug up the gaps but eventually she just emptied out. She was a paper woman, unable to fend off the storm that finally took her from us.

***

WHEN THE WORLD and my sisters are sleeping, I hear the hyenas cackle. I look through the window and I see their bone-white teeth shining in the darkness. I know that one night they will come for me but, unlike my mother, I will be ready. I pluck out my eyes and in the creeping darkness, I see everything.

Lost Jesus

MUM ALWAYS TELLS visitors she's quasi-religious whenever they comment on the large crucifix on our back wall. Mum tells us that 'quasi' means partly or almost. I guess that's why Jesus stuck around for a while, partly or almost is better that not at all.

Nobody takes much notice of Mum. Neighbours on council estates want to talk about rent arrears and sex, they don't want a discussion about whether Christ was an astronaut. She's a bit weird, our mum, wearing her flares and writing her poetry. Dad wants her to be normal. We all do. I want corned beef hash for tea not yoghurt and crisps. I want her to shut up about Jesus and aliens and to talk about Coronation Street like everyone else.

I think Dad drinks a lot because there are too many of us and the place is always a mess. Or maybe it's because Mum never wears dresses. I saw him slap her once. Right across the face. Her head flew back and banged against the kitchen door. She didn't cry though. She looked at me and said, 'Sorry, love, go to bed, it'll be okay.'

Dad gets really drunk on Sundays. He comes home

from the pub and throws the money he's won at cards on the floor. There you go, girls, he says, fight over that. Then he falls asleep in his chair, doing drunk burps. He's not sleeping today though, today he's shouting at Mum; he's furious because she's been to church.

'What the hell have you done that for? Like that's going to help. Like your God's going to come round 'ere and pay these bills.'

He's getting angrier and angrier and all I can think about is Mum's head hitting the kitchen door. Dad's chair is set against the back wall and when he kicks it back in fury, the crucifix falls on his head.

'That'll teach you,' says Mum and a miracle happens, we all start laughing, even Dad.

We found the cross later, it'd fallen down the back of the chair, but we never found Jesus. He'd come unstuck from the crucifix and his little silver body vanished forever.

Over the next few years, Mum stopped talking about Jesus and aliens, she stopped writing poetry and wearing flares. She slowly disappeared, bit by bit, until she was only partly with us – a quasi-mother creeping around the house, forever looking for her lost Jesus.

Diadem Through The Eyes Of The Bear

I CLOSE MY eyes, hoping the bear will go away, but its great paws scoop me out of bed. It's Bonfire Night and I've been sent to bed without any tea or fireworks because of the telescope. Just wait till your Dad hears about this, Mum had warned me as she closed my bedroom door.

The bear tells me to put on my clothes. 'We're going outside,' it says. I know that this is my punishment; it knows that I took its telescope without permission and broke it. The bear is going take me into the night and leave me in the woods for the tree trolls to gobble me up.

Outside, the night is alive with the pops and squeals of Bonfire Night. Despite my fear, a smile wriggles onto my lips. The bear sits down on an old bench by the side of the road and pats the seat. I climb up and wrinkle my nose; the bear smells of diesel oil and beer.

'Your grandad used to take me out on Bonfire Night and we'd sit on this bench and talk for hours.' Its eyes are glistening in the light-scratched sky. 'Does your Mum seem okay to you?'

I shrug my shoulders. When is it going to punish me?

'Never mind,' says the bear, 'Ah, now look at that, my favourite – the Diadem firework –look how it lights up the entire sky.'

I look up and see angels on fire. My breath catches in my throat. The bear holds my hand in its paw but I'm nervous of its claws. I pull away my hand and move further along the bench. I try not to see the tears shining in its eyes, reflecting the angel-fire in the sky, showing me, not the brown irises of a bear, but the soft green eyes of a man, unable to find a warm hand of a cold, November night.

Marys

THE SMELL OF over-cooked cabbage mingles with the steam rising from wet clothes drying on the maiden in front of the fire. Off-white school blouses hang there, yellow muck is still visible around the collars – Mum has been washing them by hand ever since the machine broke. Navy blue sweaters and skirts are left unwashed on our bedroom floors. They will do for another week.

I'm playing Marys with my sister, Neesy – it's a made up game where we pretend to be wives called Mary. The main point of the game is to sit on the stairs pretending to smoke pen lids and gossiping about 'that Doreen' and 'him'.

We hear him before he opens the door. The loud hiccup-burp of a drunken man is familiar to us. We scatter upstairs in unison – gazelles scenting danger. The door bangs open. I watch him through the stair rails. All I can see is the top of his head – bald but for a few ginger wisps. I watch the head float down the corridor and into the kitchen. Almost immediately the screaming starts. I am frozen. I don't want to draw attention to myself by moving.

'That bloody hurt, you swine,' Mum is saying. There's nervous laughter in her voice. I let out my breath. I hear Dad murmuring something and Mum telling him to sit down, that tea will be ready soon. There's a crash. A plate? Has Dad fallen? Is Mum alright? A door bangs open. Someone puts on the telly. It's *Bulls Eye*. I go upstairs to find Neesy. I want to play Marys.

We sit at the table to have tea. Dad stays in the front room. He has his tea on his lap. My baby sister, Carly, pushes away the greasy meat. She's too young to know what this could lead to. Neesy stares at her in horror as she begins to cry. Mum's there in a moment and whisks Carly away. We eat the rest of our tea in silence. Like a ghoul, Mum appears by Dad's side and catches his plate before it falls onto the carpet. He's fallen asleep.

Me and Neesy don't clear up the mess from the table. We don't wash the dishes. We don't fold the dried blouses and place them in our rooms. We don't help at all.

We play Marys. We play Marys and it all begins to disappear; the dirty dishes, the ragged uniforms, the desperate woman upstairs trying not to claw off her own face. We smoke our pretend cigarettes and watch the imaginary plumes swirl around the man asleep on the sofa, until he too disassembles and all that is real is the game and my sister and our make believe world of wives and women who know better.

The War Dog

WHEN THE LIGHTENING comes, it is not in the sky, it is in her eyes. I see it flash and know that thunder will follow, and I know that there is only one thing that can help us – the War Dog.

I pick up my baby sister and run upstairs; I hope Neesy will be there already. Just before I reach the top of the stairs, I dare to look back. I see the back of Mum's head as she opens the front door. There are two police officers standing on our step. I see their headless uniforms held within the frame of the door. My heart is racing. What's she done now? I was prepared for a neighbour or maybe Aunty Milly but not the police. Perhaps, this time, they will take her away.

In the back bedroom where I sleep with my two sisters, there is the War Dog. It's a large built-in wardrobe. If you go back far enough into its belly, you don't hear the shouting. It's called the War Dog because Neesy couldn't say wardrobe when we first discovered the sanctity of its walls. She's there when I open the doors. She's shuffled to the back and has covered herself in old coats.

'Here, take the baby,' I whisper-scream and she emerges from the clothes to grab Carly. I haul myself into the War Dog and shut the doors behind me.

We sit in the dark and burrow beneath old jumpers and coats. We hold hands and stare at each other; our eyes are round and black in the darkness.

The voices are muffled but Mum's voice is unmistakeable. It's loud and shrieking. The other voice, the policeman's voice, is quiet and reassuring. I can't hear her words, but I recognise the pitch. It is dangerously high. I look at Neesy. She looks scared. After the shouting there will be tears and Mum will be all soft and trembling and whispering about the taxi drivers and about how nobody believes her. We believe her. We know the taxi drivers are trying to kill her. We run with her through town when the cars are chasing her.

The front door shuts. I hear footsteps walk slowly up the stairs. I strain to hear more. Which way is she coming? I feel my sisters' fingers wrap tightly around my hands. The bedroom door opens. I hear her heavy feet walk towards us. The handle of the wardrobe moves. I pray that a nice social worker will be standing there when the War Dog opens its jaws.

'Oh girls, what are you doing in there again?' she says, and my cheeks redden with the shame of the hatred I feel as she takes the baby from my hands.

How to Make a Cup of Tea at 3am in the Morning

Ingredients

1 tea bag (must be from Kwiksave)

Sugar, the last hardened clumps at the bottom of the bag are best.

Milk – sterilised, on the turn.

Equipment

1 kettle, not electric

Tap and access to water.

Method

1. Go to sleep for approximately 5 hours.
2. Wake in the midst of a dream (nightmares are best).
3. Notice the sound of car doors slamming outside. Listen to the sound of a woman's laughter. It must be your mother's laughter for maximum effect. Hear the car's motor as it drives away.
4. Check all siblings are still sleeping.
5. Run around the house looking for your mother.
6. Cry.

7. Sit on the sofa, listening to the night-time hum of the house.

8. For extra drama, make sure you feel very scared at this point.

9. Make a decision.

10. Check on siblings again.

11. Put on a coat over your pyjamas and run to the phone box.

12. Ring your grandma. Tell her your mother has run away.

13. Do not cry on the way home.

14. Once you have worked yourself up so much you are sick, then it is time to make the tea.

15. Find the matches and light the stove.

16. Fill the kettle and place on the stove.

17. Whilst waiting for the kettle to boil, place the hardened sugar, teabag and gone-off milk into a cup.

18. Wait.

19. When you hear the kettle boil, switch off the gas and pour the hot water into the cup.

20. Stir.

21. Freeze when the door opens and your mother appears. Do not look at her dishevelled clothes and smudged lipstick.

22. Tell your mother you have rung Grandma.

23. Do not cry when her hand slaps your cheek.
24. The tea is best drunk tepid. Take to your room for maximum enjoyment.
25. Add a sprinkle of tears to enhance the flavour.
26. Drink quickly before siblings awake.
27. Hide all evidence of tea-making.
28. Trace your cold fingers over your hot, swollen cheek and do not think about how round and black her eyes were.
29. Pretend to sleep until it is time for school.

The Mother

THE DAUGHTER RUNS down the street, her nightie glistening under the mad glare of the moon. She stumbles forward, trying not to fall or cut her feet on the cold, hard stones. Her mouth and eyes are wide with terror, but another emotion is fastened to her face—anger. The daughter knows she will find no sanctuary in this place—though curtains twitch and lights flicker—nobody will open their doors for her tonight.

The Mother glides behind her—all polish and poise. Her pale and delicate hands gesticulate in the night, conducting an orchestra only she can see. The Mother does not hurry because she knows her daughter has nowhere to hide. She waves royally at the dark windows and smiles when huddled figures duck out of sight. No one can stop her tonight, not when she is in pursuit of that which has been bound to her by the laws of nature.

'Please!' screams the daughter at the faceless houses, 'For God's sake, somebody help me!'

A soft and distant echo of her own despair is the only answer to her plea.

Finally, her strength bleeds out and she falls down defeated in the street. The Mother is upon her like lichen. She presses her face close to her daughter's and she gulps down her breath and she licks off her skin and she drinks in her daughter's sweat and tears. The Mother burrows inside her and devours and devours until there is nothing left but a blood-wet nightdress and the bones of a girl who once tried to run.

A Thin Line

THE POTS ARE cracked and there are traces of coffee dirt embedded in them that, no matter how hard I scrub, I can't get rid of. I scrub them with the Brillo pads that Mum uses on the pans. I like the sound they make scraping against the porcelain; it drowns out the sound of sobbing and low whispers coming from the front room.

I should be at school, but I pretended to be ill so that I didn't have to go to English and do a presentation on Philip Larkin. I wish I'd have gone to school. I didn't think Mum was that bad but then she started howling and crawling into the dark corners of her bedroom and I had to call Aunty Milly.

Aunty Milly must have called Dad. They are both in the front room, whispering over Mum's moans and sobs. At least they've managed to get her dressed and out of her bedroom.

When Dad comes in the kitchen, I scrub harder and start sniffing noisily.

'Why aren't you at school,' he asks.

'Gos I god a cold,' I say but he's already walking out of the kitchen with a glass of water.

***

AFTER THE DOCTOR has injected Mum, after Aunty Milly has shopped and filled the cupboards with tins, after Dad has told Mum not to worry, that he'll stop drinking, they leave her with me.

In the living room, I watch my mother's body twitching on the settee. Her eyes are large and round as she stares at the ceiling. I remember a horror film where demons had ink-black eyes. The veins in my head scream when she moves her arm towards her chest and asks me to sit with her.

'Are you okay, love?' she says when I perch on the end of the sofa. I can't speak because her breath smells horrible and she's slurring her words, so I nod and try not to cry. 'I think you should stay with your Grandma for a while, just whilst you're doing your exams—it's important that you get some peace and quiet.' And then her arm flops away and her eyes droop downwards. I don't move. She looks like bones wrapped in paper. Her eyes are two dark holes and there is spit forming in the corner of her mouth.

'I hate you,' I whisper when I'm sure she's asleep. I purse my lips together and look nervously around the room, sure that I've broken some holy law about mother and daughters.

I nearly die of fright when her arm snakes back upwards and rests upon my shoulder.

'There's a thin line,' she whispers and her eyes close and she looks like my baby sister and it isn't hatred that breaks my heart into pieces.

Fly Girl

THE BELT BELONGS to Grandma. It's made of blue, shiny plastic. It instantly pulls in the drooping wool around my waist, giving my school jumper a little more shape. It doesn't help though. Malformed, black stains are forming on the jumper, climbing up my arms, creeping into the creases of my wrists, bedding themselves under my nails. Every time I scrub them away, they reappear.

I walk to school alone. My school friends live on the street where Mum and Dad and my sisters live. I guess I don't live there anymore. Grandma and Grandad live near a new estate behind my school. The houses are enormous with great rolling gardens. I like to look in the windows at the carefully stacked cushions on large, leather settees, at the mothers brushing their children's hair, smiling and unafraid.

Jane Dowling is walking behind me. She's with Amanda and Karen. I hear the familiar shriek of their laughter. I know they're talking about me. My face reddens and I walk more quickly.

'Oh my God. What is she wearing? Who puts a fucking belt on a school jumper?'

'She's trying to attract Simon Greaves.'

Shards of bright laughter explode from the girls – they impale my back. Yesterday, someone gave Simon Greaves a love letter supposedly from me. He read it to out in Geography. *Oh Simon, you make me ache between my legs…* I didn't hear the rest, I covered my ears. I hadn't written the letter. I didn't even like Simon Greaves.

'Yeah, right. The only thing she'll attract is flies. The ugly bitch. She fucking stinks.'

Jane Dowling cuffs me on the back of the head as the girls run past me. They hold their noses and pretend to vomit.

'Christ, what a smell. Where does she live? A sewer?'

When I get to school, I tell the prefect on door duty that I've started my period and need the toilet. He lets me into school early with a look of disgust on his face.

In the toilets, I take the belt off and throw it in the bin. I look in the mirror and spit at my filthy reflection. I should never have left them to deal with Mum on their own. I'm a shit sister and a coward.

I walk to Maths along the empty corridors, relishing the momentary quiet. Soon the prefects will open the doors and the school will be flooded with navy blue bodies, jostling each other, laughing at silly jokes and making fun of their teachers. As always, I will crawl into the dark places. If I'm lucky, I'll avoid the casual swats from the other kids who come to school unburdened by the sticky mess of family garbage.

A Question of Blood

IT TRANSPORTS OXYGEN and nutrients to cells which are suspended in a liquid matrix. This is called plasma. It is leaking down my legs. I feel it soaking into my socks. Red blood cells contain haemoglobin, a protein with red pigment that carries oxygen. Oxygenated or not, your blood is always red. You cannot pretend the liquid dripping down your thighs is unseen.

When Mrs Kenyon walks towards me, my body is engulfed in hot shame. I could have dealt with this. I could have sorted it out by myself. Now the entire exam hall is looking at me.

Her eyes are wet and concerned. My fist curls.

Do you need to leave? she mouths.

Fuck off, I don't reply.

I slink out of my seat, squeezing my thighs together, trying to keep the blood inside. The plastic chair is smeared brown.

In the toilet, I survey the damage. The insides of my legs are covered in red crust and I'm sore from chafing. I haven't got any sanitary towels and I haven't got enough money for the machine.

I walk out of the back entrance of school and hope Mrs Ormerod doesn't spot me from her office window. I've put both socks inside my knickers so I'm walking funny and my shoes are rubbing. I feel more blood spring up from my heels. I shuffle down the road, bleeding and crying and people move out of my way, looking at me like I'm drunk or mad. Or perhaps they can smell my shame. Shame not caused by blood but by poorness and lack. Shame that will follow me through my thin life like a mock-mouthed wraith, cruelly pointing out my bloodied body to the hyenas who prowl now, but one day will pounce.

The Long Girl

THERE ONCE WAS a girl who was so long that she couldn't fit her gangling body anywhere. She lived with a tiny family in a tiny house and every time she turned around to whirl her elongated body around, she brought the house down.

Keep still, whispered her mummy, you'll make your daddy mad.

Keep still, whispered her sisters, you're squashing us all up.

At school she tripped over her long legs and got trapped in her own long arms. It was difficult to make friends when everyone she met was an arm's length away from her. She yearned to join in the games with the other girls, but they shouted at her lolloping and tutted at her flopping appendages.

Go and sit over there with the other losers, they said.

But the other losers moved away from her because they kept getting caught up in her long fingers.

Over the years she learned how to fold herself away. At first, she tucked her feet into her shins, so she was as tall as the other girls, and then she wrapped her spindly arms around her waist like yarn until they were hardly there at all. She wound her neck down to stop her head from spiralling upwards and out into space.

Until finally she was normal sized.

But by then she couldn't stop.

She continued to reduce herself.

She became smaller than her tiny family, and her tiny school and the tiny bullies and all the tiny paper-cut words that shredded her into pieces. She became so microscopic that people forgot there had ever been a girl there at all.

Things I Can't Pack into My Suitcase

THE SMELLS OF cigarettes and Sure deodorant curling around my mum

the taste of Bird's Eye trifle every Sunday

the sound of my sisters' laughter

the bright blue colour of my socks on the day that man came to take our photograph

the smell of diesel and beer on my dad's hands

Mum's laughter when she catches us playing Marys, *What? You're all pretending to be called Mary?*

the dancing angels on the ceiling at night made by the light leaking through the door from the landing.

images of Mum pretending to hammer us into bed with her pretend hammer

our sleepy giggles at Mum and her hammer

Dad's belly laughs downstairs at something on the telly

the late-night shouting

angry voices

unnameable bangs and slaps

Mum's horror-film scream shrieking through the

house like a phantom

    my whispers under the duvet, telling my sisters to think about dancing angels

    the lace flowers on my nightie, wet with my sisters' tears

    the sounds of four little girls crying in the dark.

The Impossibility of Wings

I'M SWEATING UP a storm at the National Express bus stop. My skin feels like it's on the wrong bones. It's hot and the new baby won't stop crying and my mum's rocking her pram and smoking like a twitchy denim-clad dragon. I feel slimy and I have too many toes wriggling inside my new plastic shoes brought from Asda only hours ago.

The bus to London pulls in and the veins in my heart scream along with the air brakes. I look at Mum, she's distracted by my baby sister's sobs.

'I'm going to miss you,' I say, because that's what you say when you're leaving home – really leaving home, not just moving up the road to your Grandma's. The baby is still crying, I slick a kiss onto her forehead.

I crawl along the queue never taking my eyes off Mum who's still puffing and rocking. I don't wave when it's my turn to get on the bus. I want the other travellers to think I'm a mysterious woman, fleeing to London for unknown reasons, not just another student being waved off by her family.

Family. The word sits hard on my chest. I sneak a look through the window, she's still there. Doesn't she know she can go now? Carly and Neesy are at school, so they can't be here to say goodbye. I'm glad. The only thing worse than catching the National Express to London is being waved off by your scruffy sisters. All my friends have parents who are driving them to university.

Finally, she gives up waving and wheels the pram away from the bus, fag hanging from her mouth, curls of smoke circling her head.

I take out my Underground map and a smile creeps onto my face. I've been a caterpillar all my life and I'm finally emerging from my chrysalis. I clench my shoulders and I swear I can feel my wings unfurling with every mile we drive away from Accrington, with every mile we drive away from *her*.

***

WHAT MY SISTERS tell me at my mother's funeral:

1. The Asda shoes that Mum bought for me on the day I left for London cost £8.00. This was her entire food budget for the remaining days of the week.

2. The £100 she gave me to pay for my rent whilst I was waiting for my grant was stolen from the monthly housekeeping money.

3. She endured weeks of fighting with Dad because of this.

4. She cried for a full week after I left.

5. She never stopped talking about how proud she was of her bright, clever daughter.

***

IN BIOLOGY, WE learned that there are certain arthropods that have the external appearance of caterpillars but whose internal morphology is entirely different. By their very nature, these creatures remain bound to their shape, not only encumbered by the impossibility of wings, but unable to look up and see the true beauty of those creatures who know how to fly.

The Authors

Tom O'Brien is an Irishman living in London. He has words in numerous places including EllipsisZine, Reflex and Spelk and in print in Blood & Bourbon, Blink-Ink and DEFY! Anthologies. His novella-in-flash Straw Gods is published by Reflex Press.

Ian O'Brien writes and teaches in Manchester, UK. His work can be found online and in print via magazines and anthologies such as Neon, Prole, Fictive Dream and Storgy. He was shortlisted for the Cambridge Prize for Flash Fiction 2020.

Donna L Greenwood writes flash fiction, short stories and poetry. Her work has been nominated for Best Small Fictions and Best Microfiction. She has won several writing competitions, the most recent being Molotov Cocktail's 'Flashpocalypse'. Her most recent work in print can be found in 'The Corona Book of Ghost Stories', 'A Girl's Guide to Fly Fishing' (Reflex Press) and 'You, Me and Emmylou' (Ellipsis Zine).

Acknowledgements for The Impossibility of Wings

In the Night They Will Come for Me – *first published by Reflex Fiction January 2019*

Lost Jesus – *first published in 'You, Me and Emmylou' October 2020 by EllipsisZine*

Diadem through the Eyes of the Bear – *published in the National Flash Fiction Day Anthology 2020*

Marys – *first published in Gravel Magazine May 2019*

The War Dog – *first published in Gravel Magazine May 2019*

A Question of Blood – *first published by Idle Ink September 2020*

More from Retreat West Books

Winner Most Innovative Publisher 2020
Saboteur Awards

If you've enjoyed this book, we have many more brilliant memoirs, novels and short fiction collections from award-winning authors. Get more information at retreat-west.co.uk/books.

A Song Inside
Gill Mann

'*You are a song inside me now, a melody that stirs and bursts into life when I think of you.*'

In this heart-breaking, thought-provoking and ultimately uplifting memoir, Gill Mann remembers life with her son Sam – a boy and young man who enchanted and infuriated in equal measure. Sam saw colours where others saw grey. He made people feel alive. His unvanquishable spirit sings out as Gill reflects on the joys he brought, the difficulties of his struggles with schizophrenia, and the impact of his death.

Part journal, part journey into the past, and part conversation with Sam, in this beautifully written memoir,

Gill thoughtfully and tenderly reveals her relationship with her son, both before and after his death. *A Song Inside* explores universal issues of love and loss to reveal how we can move forward and find happiness again, without leaving behind the people we have lost.

This beautifully written and tender tribute to a beloved son is full of sadness but also of love. I learned a lot from it.'
　　—Cathy Rentzenbrink: writer, journalist and author of the Sunday Times bestselling memoir The Last Act of Love

'Sam's story is that of lots of young men: different, troubled, beloved and lost. His mother's story, and the family's, is all their own but will raise echoes for many of the process of memory, understanding and resolution.'
　　—Libby Purves: radio presenter, journalist and author

Separated From the Sea
Amanda Huggins
COSTA SHORT STORY AWARD FINALIST –
COSTA BOOK AWARDS 2018

Separated From the Sea is the debut short story collection from award-winning author, Amanda Huggins.

Crossing oceans from Japan to New York and from England to Havana, these stories are filled with a sense of yearning, of loss, of not quite belonging, of not being sure that things are what you thought they were. They are stories imbued with pathos and irony, humour and hope.

Evie meets a past love but he's not the person she thinks he is; a visit to the most romantic city in the world reveals the truth about an affair; Satseko discovers an attentive neighbour is much more than that; Eleanor's journey on the London Underground doesn't take her where she thought it would.

This is a writer who knows her craft. Never a word out of place, poignant, sometimes sad, sometimes startling, these stories fit worlds into small spaces. A long awaited debut.

—Angela Readman – author of *Don't Try This At Home*

Amanda's work is well crafted, subtle, and shows a deft hand. I love the way she gets into the psychology of each character, delving into their secret wishes and desires, giving us insights into how and why people act the way they do.

—A M Howcroft, InkTears – author of *Nobody Will Ever Love You*

The reader is transported to many different countries to experience relationships and emotions at the peak of a single moment in the characters' lives. The writing is flawless and carefully shaded, the layers of meaning unfolding elegantly.

—Joanna Campbell – author of *When Planets Slip Their Tracks*

If you want the perfect witness to a crime, Amanda Huggins is your woman. She notices everything about the people, places and the things around her. Colours, temperature, sounds, the lot. And she gets all this down in lovely little stories that spin around in the readers' head, dizzying us with her powerful images of loss, regret and yearning.

—David Gaffney – author of *All The Places I've Ever Lived*

This Is (Not About) David Bowie
FJ Morris

Every day we dress up in other people's expectations.

We button on opinions of who we should be, we insta-gram impossible ideals, tweet to follow, and comment to judge.

But what if we could just let it all go? What if we took off our capes and halos, threw away our uniforms, let go of the future. What if we became who we were always supposed to be?

Human.

This is (not about) David Bowie. It's about you.

This Is (Not About) David Bowie is the debut flash fiction collection from F.J. Morris. Surreal, strange and beautiful it shines a light on the modern day from the view of the outsider.

From lost souls, to missing sisters, and dying lovers to superheroes, it shows what it really is to be human in a world that's always expecting you to be something else.

"In This is (not about) David Bowie, FJ Morris gifts us with a five-part collection of poetry and prose and plays and hybrid works written with daring and verve and a voice that

leaps off the page. This book is as inimitable and immersive as Bowie himself, who so wisely said, "The truth is of course is there is no journey. We are arriving and departing all at the same time. "Read this collection, then everything you can find by this exciting author."

—Kathy Fish, author of *Wild Life: Collected Works from 2003-2018.*

"FJ Morris carries off with aplomb the great ask of brilliant flash fiction – that it addresses myriad subjects in a short word count. True, these stories are about David Bowie but also so much more besides. Lovers grow apart, astronauts float in tin cans, men (and women) fall to earth, fledgling explorers take their first tentative steps. Morris poetically shines a spotlight on modern life, boldly embracing different forms where lesser authors can barely manage a beginning, middle and end. A wonderful book, as imaginative as the Jean Genie himself."

—Erinna Mettler – author of *Starlings*

Unprotected
Sophie Jonas-Hill

She's fighting to save everyone else but will she have anything left to save herself? Witty, sharp and sarcastic tattoo artist Lydia's life is imploding. Her long-term relationship has broken down after several miscarriages and she's hiding from her hurt and loss in rage. After a big night out she wakes beside a much younger man who brings complications she could really do without. As her grief about her lost babies and failed relationships spirals out of control, she obsesses about rescuing a wayward teenage girl she watches from her window and gets more involved than she should with her charming but unstable young lover. *Unprotected* is a raw and punchy story of love, family and accepting yourself for who you really are.

"A raw, viscerally-beautiful gut-punch of a novel about love and loss and heartbreak and hope, and the pain we inflict on each other – and ourselves. Sophie Jonas-Hill is a powerful new voice."

—Tammy Cohen, author of *Stop At Nothing*

"Unprotected is an absorbing, thought-provoking story of betrayal and bravery. Sophie Jonas-Hill probes the darkest corners of modern society with boldness and sensitivity. I loved it!"

—Ruby Speechley, author of *Someone Else's Baby*

Remember Tomorrow
Amanda Saint

Alone. Frightened. Persecuted.

In a not-so-distant future, food is scarce, religion and superstition rule over law, and whispers about witchcraft can be more dangerous than any army. Will herbalist Evie's grandson really carry out his witch-hunting threats?

When society crumbles, activist Evie yearns to build a different kind of life. One of compassion, sustainability and equality. She doesn't expect her own family to oppose her. And when the man responsible for everything wrong in her life suddenly reappears is he there to save her – or to stop her?

Remember Tomorrow is a disturbing yet deeply moving portrait of an all-too-possible dystopian future, where family ties can fracture as easily as the world we inhabit – and the damage is not easily repaired.

"A dystopian future that echoes the present times. A reflection of society in a stark, unforgiving mirror. Unsettling, honest and unputdownable."

—Susmita Bhattacharya, author of
The Normal State of Mind

"A chilling descent into the chaos that lies in the hearts of men. A searing portrait of a dystopian future where civilisation's thin veneer has been ripped away, and it is women who suffer most as a result. Excellent."

—Paul E. Hardisty, author of
Turbulent Wake

"I enjoyed every page of Remember Tomorrow. The writing is beautifully emotive and the characters are wonderfully created. It's a world that we hope won't happen, but it's also a world that may not be too far away. Compelling, gripping and at times, deeply unsettling. Remember Tomorrow is a must read and is highly recommended by me."

—Anne Cater, book blogger, and book reviewer for
The Daily Express

Printed in Great Britain
by Amazon